Nina's Machines

Peter Firmin

A & C Black · London

WITHDRAWN

For Lucy and the boys.

CT 04233699 ₦ BR JF/C

Published 1988 by A & C Black (Publishers) Ltd
35 Bedford Row, London WC1R 4JH

Copyright © 1988 Peter Firmin

All rights reserved. No part of this publication may be reproduced, stored in a retrieval system or transmitted, in any form or by any means, electronic, mechanical, photocopying, recording or otherwise, without prior permission of A & C Black (Publishers) Ltd.

Firmin, Peter
  Nina's machines.
  I. Title   II. Series
  823'.914 [J]

  ISBN 0–7136–3060–4

Filmset by Kalligraphics Ltd, Redhill, Surrey
Printed in Great Britain by
William Clowes Ltd, Beccles and London

If you travelled,
by plane perhaps,
to the top of Italy,

and sailed, in a
motor boat, maybe,

across the rough seas from the coast,

3

and managed, perhaps by hovercraft,
to cross the weedy reedy marshes,

then you'd come to an island
with just one hill.

And if you climbed those grassy slopes, right to the top, you could look down,

if you didn't feel too dizzy, and see a small town at the foot of the other steeper side.

To reach the town you'd have to

scramble down a dusty track,

zig-zagging through the olive trees

past an old
stone house.

Well, once upon
a time, an inventor
lived in that house.
He was called
Old Orlando and the
house was
his workshop.

Old Orlando

Down below in the town, lived a girl called Nina. Nina had a cat.

Now Nina couldn't cross the marsh by hovercraft or sail across the sea by motor boat. She couldn't fly in a plane to other countries. Because this was hundreds of years ago before any of these things had been thought of, let alone invented.

Every day,
Nina climbed the
winding path

up to the workshop
to bring bread and milk

for Orlando and his
four apprentices, Ricardo,
Alfonso, Mario and Roberto.

The boys did his drawings
and made his models.

From the top of the hill, Nina
watched the birds, the seagulls and
crows, flying across the marshes
and over the sea
to the mainland.

What a hope!
In those days girls
fetched and carried. They swept and
cleaned. But inventing – never!

Old Orlando's workshop was over-run with mice. Now wouldn't you think that a great inventor could get rid of a few mice? He did try.

He made clever cages, baited with delicious Italian cheese. The mice couldn't resist it.

But they were clever. They stole the cheese without ever getting caught.

And they hardly noticed the mouse-scarers with flashing eyes and screechy voices. They just squeaked back and carried on nibbling.

Screech

squeak!

I can't stand their beady eyes and wiggling tails

It became so bad that even the cleaner left and refused to come back until all the mice had gone.

So Orlando set his boys a competition.

All the usual work was put aside and by Saturday night four sheets of drawings were stacked in the studio waiting to be judged.

1
Roberto's step Trap.

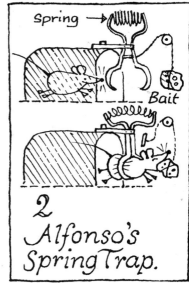

2
Alfonso's Spring Trap.

The Four Inventions

3
Mario's Fast Bonker.

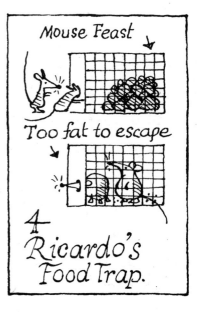

4
Ricardo's Food Trap.

But during Saturday night . . .

Sunday morning . . . disaster! The drawings were in a thousand pieces. The mice had chewed them up.

'Rampaging Rodents!' screamed Old Orlando. 'They must have known what we were planning. Get someone to clear up the mess.'

One of the boys, Roberto, lived next door to Nina.

'Would you like to work in our workshop?' he asked her.
'Oh yes,' she said. 'I'd love to invent things. I'll invent a flying machine.'

'You can start tomorrow,' said Roberto. 'Cleaning and sweeping.'
'Oh!' said Nina.

On Monday morning she went up
to Orlando's workshop. She swept
and dusted and cleared up the mess.

The boys spread out their papers
and talked about mousetraps.
Nina listened.

Next day she took her cat to work.
'No animals!' yelled Old Orlando.
He didn't know about cats.

Nina's cat was the only one
on the island. But that
cat knew about mice!

She leapt out of Nina's basket,
dashed behind cupboards,

up the stairs, under the bed
and into the kitchen

and before you could say
"Cat's Whiskers!" every
mouse had bitten the dust.

Orlando was delighted.

'How much?' he said.

'Not for sale,' said Nina.

'Definitely not!'

'But we need a cat,' whined Orlando.

'Where can we get one?'

'There's not another on the island,'
said Nina, 'mine is the only one.'

'Well then,' said the inventor,
'kittens. She must have kittens and
I'll keep one . . . or two.'
'Oh, you silly old inventor,' said
Nina. 'Didn't you hear me? She's
the only one. To have kittens you
have to have two: a mummy and a
daddy . . . Didn't you know that?'

That's when Nina realised that the
old inventor wasn't quite as bright
as he made out.

That's when she made her PLAN.
She agreed to stay, with the cat . . .

... just for six weeks,
but on one condition.

Yes, yes, what's that?

Starting next week
you let me do a little
real work — you know,
inventing and drawing
and all that...

25

'Oh, very well,' said Orlando, 'but we work an eight hour day. You'll do the cleaning for the rest of the time.' Old Orlando really wanted that cat around.

Nina smiled to herself. Old Orlando stared at her, suspiciously – but he didn't guess her plan.

Nina swept and cleaned.

'Now what shall we find for you to do,' Orlando mumbled through the clouds of dust, 'in your fifteen minutes?'

'Oh, don't be silly,' said Orlando, 'something to get rid of all this dust would be more useful.

Nina didn't argue. Fifteen minutes a day wasn't really enough time to invent a flying machine.
But a sweeping machine . . .
that was no trouble.

She'd finished by Friday morning and the boys were put to work making Nina's . . .

The boys couldn't wait to try it out.

Next week while Nina was fetching
water from the waterfall, they took
turns sweeping and cleaning, so
that when she came back there was
just the cooking and washing to do.

When it was time to do her
HALF HOUR of drawing . . .

Shall I work on my flying machine?

No!

'Birds fly, and bats,'
said Orlando.
'Even some fish
fly, but not people.
I've watched you fetching water;
scrambling over the rocks from the
waterfall. You can invent something
to do that job.'

It took the boys a little longer to make her second invention: Nina's . . .

Self-emptying Water Transporter

Waterfall

Empty buckets

Full buckets

Paddle

They even stayed over the weekend to finish it.

On Monday they all had showers.

'Oh, that flying machine,' groaned Old Orlando.

He looked at all the boys' dirty clothes. They had been working hard and it was very dusty on the hillside.

'A machine for washing clothes,' he said. 'Now that would be useful.'

See to it, Nina.

Bossy old man!

She had ONE HOUR a day
that week to
invent her . . .

Donkey-powered Washing Tub

It was rather big.

But it worked.

and it could even do the dishes

without breaking too many.
The boys were so keen to use the washing tub that they asked if their mothers could use it too.
Orlando sighed . . .

Oh well, let them all come.

He watched all the women trudging up the hill under their bundles of washing.

He was so busy putting up washing lines that he forgot to give Nina a job.

So that week, with TWO HOURS each day at the drawing board, Nina invented something to get her home quicker. It was Nina's . . .

Foot-powered Riding Machine

Passenger Seat ↓

Driver Seat ↓

Steering handle ↓

Basket for Cat ↘

Leather band to drive back wheel

foot pedals

(or as you would call it, her bike).

'That's useful,' said Orlando, and he let Roberto help her make it. By Saturday afternoon it was finished, so with Roberto on the back and her cat in the basket they . . .

whizzed . . .

down the winding track to their homes in the town.

But Monday morning it was a different story. Pushing that heavy bike up the steep hill was really tough work, so they were late for work.

Orlando was waiting at the top.
'Down is easy,' he said. 'We need
something for "Up". Something to
lift us up the steep cliff. A cliff-lift,
that's what you must do this week.

A flying machine
would do the same.

'No, no,' said Orlando. 'All week I've been watching those poor ladies struggling up the hill. They could use a cliff-lift too.'

Off to work, Nina.

She had FOUR HOURS
each day to work on her:

Water-powered Cliff-Lift

winding gear

engaging lever

paddle

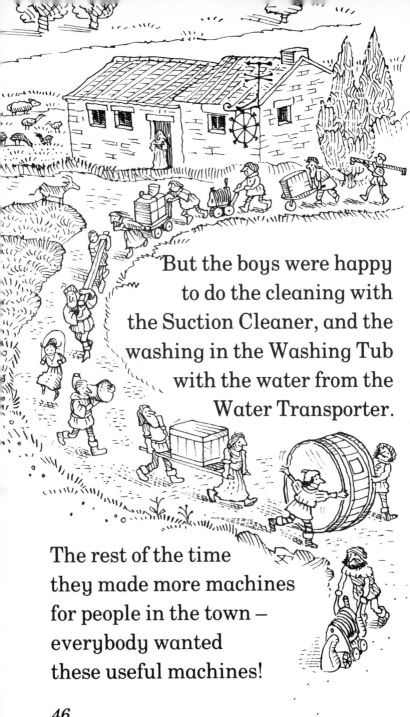

But the boys were happy
to do the cleaning with
the Suction Cleaner, and the
washing in the Washing Tub
with the water from the
Water Transporter.

The rest of the time
they made more machines
for people in the town —
everybody wanted
these useful machines!

So Nina spent the other four hours cooking some really amazing meals for them all.

Oh, dear

When he saw her drawings, Orlando started worrying about all the time it would take to make this great lift.

Orlando was persuaded.

All next week he was busy helping the boys to build the lift down the cliff.

All except Roberto who was working
with Nina, for EIGHT HOURS each
day on . . .

something else.

When they'd finished the lift
Old Orlando went up and down it
several times a day.
Sometimes he went up and down
just for fun. Sometimes he went into
town to see his friends which he
hadn't done for many a day
because of his old legs.

And sometimes
he went shopping.

He had plenty of
money for new clothes

Orders for machines
were coming in from
all over the island –

and the lift
had become a
great attraction.

Customers paid to come up on the
lift, and the machines they bought
went down on the lift.

Old Orlando, the great inventor,
strutted around in his new clothes
in his busy, clean workshop.
He'd almost forgotten about Nina.
One day, Nina came up to him.

'Goodbye!' he said. 'But you can't leave us now. Not when everything is going so well.'

'Yes, said Nina. 'Anyhow,
my cat hasn't seen a
mouse for weeks, and she's
feeling a bit restless.'

'Ah, yes, the cat,' said Orlando. 'She certainly was the best mouse trap ever. The prize is five gold pieces.'
'They will be useful,' said Nina.
'To pay for my new workshop.'

'But what about this flying
machine?' croaked Orlando.
'Roberto!' Nina called. 'You can
bring it out now.'

Roberto, Mario, Alfonso and Ricardo
dragged out the flying machine.

The bike was part of it and
flaps were fixed to the wheels.
On top were two great wings
of cane, leather and silk.

In front, of course, there was a basket for the cat.

I must fly..

They wheeled it out to the edge of the hill facing across the sea to the mainland.

Old Orlando just stood there, with
his mouth hanging open.
Nina pedalled away down the
grassy slope, until the wind caught
the wings, and the machine lifted
into the air.

Then she engaged the
flapping gear and flew.

Yes, Nina flew the amazing
flying machine over the reedy,
weedy marsh and up and away
across the sea towards the
distant land.